DATE DUE

FEB 1 5 1995	NOV 2 2 1996	
FEB 2 9 1995	MAR 1 9 1997	
MAR 1 5 1995		
MAR 2 4 1995	MAY 1 6 1997	
APR 3 1995	JUN 4 1997	
APR 2 5 1995	AUG 1 9 1997	
MAY 5 1995	OCT 2 5 1997	
MAY 2 4 1995	SEP 3 0 1998	
JUN 3 1995	JUN 8 1999	
JUN 3 0 1995	MAR 2 7 2000	
JUL 1 4 1995	SEP 0 9 2000	
SEP 1 1995	NOV 2 9 2000	
	SEP 1 4 2001	
MAR 8 1996	DEC 2 8 2001	
APR 2 1996		
NOV 6 1996		

jj

HAAS, JESSIE

BUSYBODY BRANDY

95-100

BUSYBODY BRANDY

By **Jessie Haas**

Pictures by **Yossi Abolafia**

 Greenwillow Books, New York

Watercolor paints and a black pen were used for the full-color art.
The text type is Avant Garde.
Printed in Hong Kong by South China Printing Company (1988) Ltd.
First Edition 10 9 8 7 6 5 4 3 2 1

Library of Congress Cataloging-in-Publication Data
Haas, Jessie.
Busybody Brandy / by Jessie Haas ; pictures by Yossi Abolafia.
p.   cm.
Summary: Brandy, a farm dog, is busy day and night.
ISBN 0-688-12792-4 (trade).   ISBN 0-688-12793-2 (lib. bdg.)
(1. Dogs—Fiction.   2. Domestic animals—Fiction.)
I. Abolafia, Yossi, ill.   II. Title
PZ7.H1129Bu   1994   (E)—dc20
93-29569   CIP   AC

To Michael and his dog —J. H.
To Duba —Y. A.

Brandy is a farm dog. Her day starts early.

When the sky is getting gray, the rooster wakes
the sun up. *COCK-A-DOODLE-DOOO!*
Brandy helps the rooster.
AAaa-rrrr-OOoooo! Rooo-aaowoo-oooo!
COCK-A-DOODLE-DOO-OO!
Busybody dog! I can do this by myself!

The hens are laying eggs now.

Buck-buck-buck-buck-bu-G A W K !

I got one, I got one, I got one!

Brandy runs to the henhouse. She helps the
hens tell about their eggs. Rruff! Rruff! Rruff!

Buck-buck-busybody! Busybody dog!

We don't need you!

The squirrels are stealing grain.

Chuk-chuk-chu-chuk-chuk!

Chuk-chuk-chu-chuk! It's over here! Here!

Brandy chases them onto the roof.

Rrarf! Rrarf! Stay up there! You can't have that!

Bu-bu-bu-busybody! Bu-bu-bu-busybody dog!

The sheep must go to a new pasture.
Brandy helps the farmer drive them.
Maa-aa-ind your own business!
Maaind your own business! Busybody!

The cat has kittens.
Brandy wants to kiss them.
Ssstay away! Sscram! Busssybody!

The farmer goes to get the hay. Brandy
helps load it. On the wagon, off the wagon,
on the wagon, off the wagon.
"Oh, Brandy! What a busy dog!"

Night is coming. Hens in the henhouse.
Brandy puts them in.

Buck-buck-busybody!

Sheep in the sheep pen.

Maaind your own business!

Kittens in the hayloft.

Sstay out! Sscram!

Squirrels in the treetops.
Bu-bu-bu-busybody! Busybody dog!

The sun goes to bed.
The farmer goes to bed.
Brandy goes to bed, too.
But she does not go to sleep.

The weasel creeps up to the henhouse.
Brandy smells him. Woof woof! Beat it!
Busybody dog!

The coyote sneaks around the sheep pen.
Brandy hears him. Woofwoofwoof!
Get out of here!
Busybody!

The fox slinks up to the hay barn.

But Brandy is watching.

Woof! Woof! Stay away! Scram!

Busybody dog!

The farmer turns in bed.
"Good dog, Brandy."

Everything is still.

The long day is over.

Brandy closes her eyes, and she sleeps.